Chakras, Meridians, and the Color Energies

By Patsy Stanley

ISBN 978-1-7326193-6-4

LCCN 2018908826

This is basic information for studying the Spiritual Nature of life as it applies to Metaphysical Studies.

Human was once spelled Hue-Man...

We live our lives in the presence of an Infinite and Eternal Energy that is constantly forwarding itself. All we have to do to know this is to look around us. We live within, and are surrounded by, the life force we are a part of.

When we look out from the Earth, we can see the Great Cosmic Seas and the Stars we were made from, birthing and dying, and Etheric Spirit waiting in the empty spaces to be born. We are a part of all of that. Those are our processes too, for we carry the same identity and patterning the universe does. Very impressive!

Each planet out there in the Cosmos has its own laws of manifestation that the Dual Nature of Motion and Matter of the life occurring on that planet must follow. Each planet is a living entity with its own Elemental Nature and set of Color energies (Motion) it must follow. There are definite hierarchies of Beings that govern these things on each planet. Some of these hierarchies are very old, in terms of time as we know it.

The energies Earth uses, this living planet we are born onto, come from the Universe. Human beings are made of those same energies. The sun emits radiation. The moon emits magnetism and several other energies. The planets and stars and dying stars and others out there, emit their own energies. The Earth is constantly being bathed in many different vibrations of these cosmic energies. Those different vibrations call forth by law, connection and manifestation within and without each Hue-man to those cosmic energies.

And so we continue. We are under at least the third Moon and the third sun in this latest era of human kind. The Earth has been swept clean of humans at least ten times and reseeded according to the Planetary Councils that Inform the Majesty of Planetary Plentitude.

Because we are made of the Earth, the Sun and the Stars, the seeded histories of humanity carry the same genetic cosmic coding that is being/has been forwarded since the Big Bang.

The Reflectors of this lie in the great Outer Realms of Form and are Visioned to humans as the Great Sun, The Adept Moon, and The Seedling Earth. Many more ages will pass before Hue-mans understand the purposeful stabilization that takes place on their behalf through these Three Sacred Entities.

The colors / light / proton present in every atom of humanity and in everything else, are different names representing the masculine nature of life.

In this book, we will be studying the color energies and how they work.

Colors emit in waves. Electro-magnetic radiation is responsible for the colors we see.

A Brief History of Light

About two thousand years ago, Light began to be associated with spiritual growth. This came about in China, where books had been recorded for over a thousand years. Mo Tze was a military genius, who prevented much violence in his day. He left behind a collection of essays propounding universal love, non-violence, and the ending of poverty and blind obedience to authorities.

A few hundred years later, the first emperor assumed complete authority over thought and what it should be, and gave China its name. The great philosophers' books were burned, and the Chinese people were forced to give up all free thinking for the next one thousand years. The study of spirit and its relationship to light was stopped for that time.

In the eleventh century, the golden age of science began in the Islamic world in Iraq, led by Ibn AL Hazen. All religions were welcomed. Books were searched out from all over the world and preserved. Much of the ancient knowledge we have today exits because of his efforts. The rules of scientific methodology we use today were put in place back then.

Zero and its operation were first defined by Hindu astronomer and mathematician Brahmagupta in 628.

The first recorded example of astronomy is around 3,500 years old and comes from Mesopotamia. Babylonian writings and star charts mapped out the sky, as well as made constant references to the names of stars given to them by the Sumerians This implies they were probably observing the night sky in the early Bronze age. Confirmation of the earliest astronomers are tricky to find, as we believe that people have always studied the sky in one way or another.

Science and Light in the Western world:

Isaac Newton was the first to study light and give us our modern understanding of the rainbow. In 1691, Newton, using a prism to separate light, propounded the theory of a color spectrum and named the seven colors. (He named the seven color energy aspects of the masculine Nature.)

He chose the seven colors out of a belief derived from an ancient group of Greek teachers called Sophists, who believed that the color energies had a spiritual nature, that colors were connected to music notes, to the objects in our solar system, and to the days of the week.

History of the Chakra Philosophy

The study of the chakras and their systems are Philosophies and Spiritual studies; they are contained in the Vedas – spiritual books which came to us from ancient India. This philosophy is the most ancient concept known to humanity of how our energy works through our personal energy systems to achieve spiritual "enlightenment".

The first known description of the chakra system was written in the Upanishads. This philosophy of how energy systems work first appeared in the Upanishads, or The Indian Scriptures, as far back as the first millennium, BCE. (Before Christian Era). The different parts of the Chakra Philosophies were composed over several centuries, and in various regions of India. The latest Indian scripture was written in the Medieval Period. The Greeks also propounded a type of chakra system. In the eighth century, Buddhism introduced their orderly hierarchy system of chakras.

The book of the Upanishads is considered to be one of the most influential books ever written. These Spiritual Philosophies were first printed in the Sanskrit language, one of the oldest languages on the planet.

The Vedas, which are the four ancient collections of Indian hymns and formulas containing these philosophies, were translated from the Sanskrit in 1657. The title given to the earliest translation was "The Greatest Mystery", and they remain just that, for only parts of the information needed to make the whole, are contained in the books.

The Veda teachings traveled from India into Persia, (the successive states of Iran before 1935 were collectively called Persia.), then into France, where it was translated into French and Latin. Many famous German philosophers gave the Veda teachings great recognition beginning in 1819, and they spread throughout Europe. In America, the "Vedic Scriptures" became popular through authors Thoreau and Emerson.

There are spiritual systems of study that say chakras are like lotus blossoms. Other spiritual systems say there are more than seven chakras. All of the spiritual systems that study chakras agree that chakras open slowly, spin faster, and enlarge as we evolve.

Different spiritual texts and teachings believe in different numbers of chakras as well as their locations. Different cultures with varying genetics, list the chakra energy systems and how they operate according to how it works for their genetic system.

The most popular belief about how color energies work spiritually in the western world, is the Shakta Theory, introduced in 1927 into the western world by Arthur Avalon in his book, "The Serpent Power", where he describes seven Major chakras. Avalon was a British orientalist, whose many works helped to bring about a deep and wide interest in the Hindu and Yoga philosophies.

Other books have also been written about chakras. These include:

- ¬ John Woodroffe wrote The Serpent Power in 1927.
- ¬ Leadbeater wrote his book, "The Chakras" in the early 1930's.

At that point, the interest in the Veda teachings died down and remained in the Mystery school teachings until the 1960's, when the Vedic-Chakra-Spiritual philosophies were brought back to the west from the gurus in India, and shared publicly with the western world. No longer was this information, known for centuries in the eastern world, only available to a select few in the western world.
Today those Eastern philosophies have become the basic template for many of the Western holistic, alternative healing methods, as well as a spiritual directive for many seeking a path leading to spiritual enlightenment.

How the chakras open

In the Yogic Spiritual philosophy, (Hindu-Yogatattva Upanishad-around 400 BCE) spiritual enlightenment and development is pursued by activating and awakening the chakras. The chakras in each of the bodies open the self through meditations, mantras, and pursuing the personal betterment and understanding of the self. As the chakras open, they allow an awakening of more awareness to whole areas of Life and an understanding the person has never experienced before.

Most of the Eastern philosophies and religions believe that to the degree that our chakras are open; that is the extent to which we know our God. Their disciplines are based on mantras and meditations, which give receptivity to opening these energy transformer centers. In the Eastern philosophies, it is believed that it is in the giving up of the doing that one comes to know their God.

In the Western philosophies, it is believed that it is in the doing that one comes to know their God. Both philosophies focus on opening the chakras.

It is said that the seven chakras correspond to the glands of the endocrine system. Edgar Cayce said that the seven churches in the Book of Revelations in the Christian Bible represent the endocrine glands, thus the seven chakras.

Chakras

"Chakra" is the Sanskrit word referring to an ancient concept of the spinning wheels of light, the circular shaped energy vortexes existing in the surface of the Etheric double in humankind.
Chakras are the dispersal systems for the color energies that pour into and out of the human body, providing the vital life force to it. In some spiritual practices, these chakra centers are referred to as lotus blossoms.

The Meridian Grid Systems

Since ancient times, Chinese philosophies of healing have used the grid system to map the meridian structures, and use them as a foundation for healing. They have graphed the meridian crossings and lines over the physical body, and studied them for spiritual, physical, and psychological qualities, both negative and positive.

Everything is made of sound. Wherever a major and minor sound crosses each other, intersects, harmonics or sound takes place, creating spinning spheres. Here is where the sacred music begins. We are made of Music and it all begins here. We are made of sound. Colors and Elements come together and create sound energies.

In the meridian grid system, the colors and elements intersect, and at that intersection, they create a vortex of both positive and negative energies, an electro-magnetic life force zone, that creates a neutral, spinning disc. And in this neutral zone, the energies are received from and released back into the system, over and over again. Energy is relayed back and forth constantly between these minor chakra centers and the Major chakra centers.

These crossing points are said to be the seat of our three dimensional consciousness. Each of the chakras these grids are connected to, governs whole aspects of living. These basic color energies and their sounds, coincide with the Light teachings in most spiritual, religious, and esoteric Orders today.

"The Nei Ching" from China, uses the meridian grid structure. It says the grid intersections occur every inch and a half. It is the first documented medical book, and is still in use today. Out of these ancient studies have come holistic and alternative medicine advances, such as pain control techniques, acupuncture, and acupressure, and many other healing techniques.

The chakra and meridian system in the bodies:

The seven chakras sit from the top of the head down to the base of the spine. Chakras run along and adjacent to our nervous system. The nervous system runs from the base of the spine in bundles of twelve up into the head, where they connect and go into the brain.
The nerves are in charge of and connected to the skeletal system and the muscle system. The nervous system processes the faster body energies. The endocrine system processes the slower body energies.

The nervous system is our communication network. Our nerves oversee the reception of all kinds of communication, including our emotional, spiritual, and mental thought processes, and the messages the universe we are a part of, is constantly sending us, so that we can stay a part of it.

Chakras spin in a clockwise, circular motion. They are the dispersal systems for the color energies throughout all of our physical, mental, astral, and soul bodies. They send the color energies out along the meridian system into the rest of the bodies.

The chakras are spinning vortexes of energy that allow the life force to travel the energy pathways called meridians. There are twelve major meridians, and they are attached to the Chakras that run from the base of the spine to the top of the head and around the cranial plates.

In the upper occipital ridge, there are five major centers carried in the head, aside from the crown chakra. These chakras are aligned with the cosmic chakras that spin around our heads.

The Meridians are energy pathways. They feed their energy into the chakras, and are sent their energy from the chakras.

We receive the energy and experience the self through the magnetic, elemental energies working with that color. The energy is then released back out into the meridian system and it is carried back into the chakra to be expressed through the color energies. Chakras bathe and fuel the organs in their area. They govern each gland in the endocrine system and carry information about the person to all parts of the self.

Chakras process each of our body's experiences through expression. Each Chakra is seven layers deep, the elements (Kingdom) in that area keeping the innermost in contact with the outermost.

Chakras open slowly, spin faster, and enlarge as we evolve.

Chakras convert and calibrate light/matter energy into energy we can assimilate in our bodies. Energy is too fast moving and too pure for us to survive without the chakra and meridian intervention system. Each chakra governs a specific part of life. They are energy transformers for the many aspects of living we do through our conscious awareness.

Energy

The energy comes in through the chakra network then it is sent out along the meridian structures. The meridians look like physical blood vessels, capillaries, except they carry energy instead of physical fluids.

The receptor part of the nerve picks up the energy. The energies that are slower in vibration, the less refined energies, are sent into the lower chakras. Each chakra takes in energy according to the vibration rate of the energy. The vibration rate become faster because it loses density as it moves up through the chakras. Therefore, the colors change because they are working with different elements, therefore, different Elemental Kingdoms. Each of our energy bodies residing on the different energy planes have different densities.

Each body has to receive and process the energies that vibrate at the rate it needs to survive.
The red root chakra receives the slowest vibratory energy and is aligned with the physical body. The violet crown chakra receives the fastest vibratory energy. You're up to the soul planes at that point.

Character Development

The Principle of Radiation sends the Light out that radiates out in all directions, out of which all forms of separation and expansion, all occurring constantly everywhere in the universe, galaxy, cosmos, and on our planet, take place.

To develop and express one's self, to individuate, requires the color energies, because at some time on the path you walk, you have to individuate in order to evolve. The intention is to separate you, so that a part of yourself can evolve.

Separation is the only way that evolutionary processes can take place. Connection is the only way involution can take place.

One has to learn about and work with both the Color and Elemental Energies at the same time, or you will throw yourself out of balance in a serious way. You become too acidic (colors) or too alkaline (elements) and can end up with the major problems that go with being out of balance.

The understanding of the Elemental Kingdoms remain under the Protection of the Elemental Hierarchies. These Kingdoms govern the evolution of character development. For example, the green bean is at the top of the hierarchy in its Kingdom. This is organic spirituality and can't be laughed off without a loss.

To access the Elemental Kingdoms, one must go through the stages of character development. Questions and answers change as we develop our conscious awareness to include more of life. This is a long process that has to take place in stages, for we are working with the evolution of all of the parts of the self.
Each chakra works in association with an Elemental Kingdom developed and maintained through the electron, the magnetic force of Matter, the other half of the life force in every atom of life. The male/proton/color always works with the female/electron/element.

In the meridian grid, (some say every inch and a half, some say less) the colors and elements intersect, and at that intersection, they create a vortex of both positive and negative energies, an electro-magnetic life force zone that creates a neutral, spinning disc. And in this neutral zone, the energies are received from and released back into the system, over and over again.

There are both major and minor chakra intersections. Energy is relayed back and forth constantly between these minor chakra centers and the Major chakra centers.

Colors/male and Elements/female come together and create sound energies. Everything is made of sound, including us.

Wherever a major and minor sound crosses each other, or intersects, harmonics or sound takes place, creating spinning spheres. These points are said to be the seat of our three dimensional being. Each chakra these grids are connected to, governs whole aspects of living. These basic color energies and their sounds, coincide with the Light teachings in most spiritual, religious, and esoteric Orders today.

Learning about character development is slow, serious work that brings more responsibility. The color energies are easier to work with, they are fun and quick, and many people choose them because of this, but there is no easy fix. The work has to be done. Issues, or problems, are strategically located Matter residing near specific intersections to insure the pacing of that person's character development. This placement of Matter is no accident. These issues or problems, are the Matter that provides the frequencies we have to have in order to manifest here and stay on the planet.

Too much "enlightenment?" We leave the planet. We have to have Matter, which manifests as issues in our lives, to stay here. Those issues are calibrated to the lessons we have to learn in this classroom of Life. We have to have something to work on. Our experiences are provided through the Elements and are specific to our issues (matter).

Everything we have ever experienced and not expressed throughout our eternal life, is still waiting to be expressed.

As we evolve and grow, we earn the right to develop character attributes. This access is provided through the Elemental kingdoms and their association with the Color energies. This is how the larger, better, more refined aspects of our human character are developed, so our Higher Nature can kick in and run our show.

The Color Brotherhoods

The higher vibrational aspects of the Color energies, Light, Motion, and Expression, are administered and overseen through the Color brotherhoods. These brotherhoods work with the structural aspects of the masculine Nature on planet Earth.

Definition of Light

Light is a form of energy, and while it can easily be changed into other forms of energy, it cannot be destroyed. While absorption by an opaque material seems to destroy it, it is actually converted into heat absorption.

Definition of Dark

Dark is a form of energy lacking light or brightness, and while it can be changed into other forms of energy, it cannot be destroyed.

After Light began to be associated with spiritual growth, eventually, the spiritual Brotherhoods of Light and the Sisterhoods of the Elements were assigned.

Every atom in existence contains at least one proton, an electron, and a neutron. The masculine force of radiance and expansion that sends away and separates and projects is the proton.

They are the energies through which all separation, radiation, expansion, and communication in all of its forms, takes place throughout our universe.

The seven major color energies rotate around the proton, and are called leptons. The seven color energies express the Principle of Radiance in seven different ways.

Many spiritual teachings describe the seven sacred paths. In esoteric teachings, these paths are often described as soul Rays (Brotherhoods) or temperaments. The activities and values of each color ray system form the Color Brotherhoods.

All beings, humans, plants, animals, rocks, etc., work with a primary Ray and with secondary Rays.

The color energies develop the energies of Knowledge. It is through the color energies that we experience all Individuation. It is through them that we see ourselves as separate from others, a necessary thing. This is how we evolve. Evolution occurs for us through the opening and individualization of the chakras. The involution necessary to us so that we stay connected during the evolutionary process, comes from the Elements.

There are seven Color Brotherhoods that make up the light that shines in each atom of our being.

The Color Brotherhoods define the personality structure, for the Brotherhoods are about Individuation, which is manifested through the development of personality.

Each Color Brotherhood provides for and governs different spiritual characteristics:

Black Brotherhood

- ϖ The Black Brotherhood governs the Magnetic Principle of Fusion in the Life Force.
- ϖ They invoke and maintain the Great Karmic Principle that all of life operates under, not only the physical laws that we humans might perceive the tip of, but all of the laws that all parts of life operate under.

- ϖ The Black Brotherhood is responsible for the delivery of Karma, for Karma is magnetic. Karmic Principles, delivery of Karma, brings order out of chaos.
  - o These Principles alert all parts of life as to how far off their path they are, by the laws of contraction. Contraction is the Cause that creates the effects of fear or pain.

- o The Black Brotherhood works with the Karmic boards to alert you as to how far off your path you are — through sending pain — the worse it gets, the harder it is to stay off your path.
- ϖ Many Pagans work with the Black Brotherhood because it governs Spirituality manifesting into Matter.
  - o The Pagan personality is most like the Black Brotherhood personality.
  - o They work predominantly with the Elements
  - o They are attracted to Mysteries, good listeners who read more into what you are saying than you realize, slower and more deliberate than most other people, a different set of joyful values that are hard for people who work predominantly with the color energies to understand.
  - o Negatively, they may be prone to depression, and to aimlessness

White Brotherhood

- ϖ Encompasses all the Brotherhoods except the Black, and is the governing system for all of them.
- ϖ They govern all the color hierarchies and boards.
- ϖ They disseminate information to the other brotherhoods and initiate into the White Brotherhood.
- ϖ They govern the chain of command and the governing boards, and they keep the planet on course.
- ϖ The White Brotherhood personality is all about structure and they are absolutely goal oriented.
- ϖ They govern all initiations and rites of passage.
- ϖ Their compassion is in going before you to prepare the way.
- ϖ They know how to sacrifice for the good of the ego.

- ϖ Negatively, they can be extremely rigid and proud, manipulative, a lack of boundaries with no respect for the effect they have on others lives, because they feel that no one knows as much as they do.

- ϖ They are regal, take over, and talk too much. They need to be the star of the show. They are above everyone around them. They are the only teacher in town.

The White Brotherhood puts it all together, White works with Integration, Black with Connection.

Red Brotherhood

- ϖ Red is the color of the First Ray Soul.
- ϖ The Root This Brotherhood says, "I am!" in conjunction with, "I will!"
- ϖ They are learning about God through the physical world, which is directly linked to Divine Will and Personal Will, Courage, and physical Strength.
- ϖ Red is the path of Divine Will and works with the Spiritual aspects of Divine Will. It is the path of" I", of learning about dynamic leadership and pioneering.
- ϖ It is the energy that takes raw materials and builds a basic, unrefined structure for the future from it.
- ϖ The pioneers who settled America are one example of this kind of energy. Construction workers and athletes work with red. People who work with red are Earth Warriors.
- ϖ They tend to be active physically and to be very grounded. People who work with red like confrontation. They can be short sighted and impatient.
- ϖ First ray souls support individuality-red – insists on one committing to one's self — are highly personal and challenging.

Orange Brotherhood

ϖ Orange is the color of the second ray soul.

ϖ They work with the principle of Union.

ϖ They strive for unity, whether it is negative or positive.

ϖ Orange people work with vitality, feeling, astral body, desire, wants, all aspects of union, and the essence of life in its transformational stages.

ϖ The second ray soul uses bursts of indignation to change something socially for them, because the second and seventh chakra people are love patrons of the heart.

ϖ Negatively, can be indiscriminate about sexual choices

Yellow Brotherhood

ϖ Yellow is the color of the third ray soul.

ϖ These people learn acceptance through objectivity, through let it be, and structure.

ϖ They work with logic, the sciences, the mental body, business, thought, scientists, the skeletal structure, and bones and teeth.

ϖ Are objective in the face of high emotions.

ϖ They can seem cold, and get too far away from sympathy and emotions for self or others. Too objective.

Green Brotherhood

ϖ Green is the color of the fourth ray soul.

ϖ This is the shield brotherhood

ϖ Works with all shields, shielding and harmony, balancing of the planet
  o has both positive and magnetic aspects of energy.

ϖ Easily excited. Very emotional, wears their heart on their sleeve, can be overemotional, musical, and visual

Blue Brotherhood

ᚦ Blue is the color of the fifth ray soul.

ᚦ They use peaceful, calm, tranquil, communication

ᚦ The Catholic church is a blue brotherhood path.

ᚦ The blue brotherhood is the path of devotion and devotees. All confronts are given back over to the guru. You do not question the leader. They will tell you what you are supposed to do and aspire to in life. You are committed to the religion and the guru and express your life through their guidance. This path is the path of beginning development of higher philosophy. Christians, Yogis, Catholics to mention a few. Calm, detail oriented, deliberate, graceful movements, dislikes loud people, and loud noises. Can be nitpickers.

Indigo Brotherhood

ᚦ Indigo is the color of the sixth ray soul.

ᚦ Changes in vibrations of matter can occur here.

ᚦ Addictions have to be addressed.

ᚦ Ancestors begin to be addressed.

ᚦ Histories and their details are important to these people.

ᚦ Understanding of how things came to be.

ᚦ Give too many details for most people.

Violet brotherhood

ᚦ Violet is the color of the seventh ray soul.

ᚦ They are beginning to examine collective truths.

ᚦ Members have moved past the guru stage and are beginning to create their own God self.

ᚦ Serious personality, not much humor, connects back to the higher spiritual principle of "Unity- I Am One".

ᚦ A great interest in higher teaching and learning of magic and rituals, developing the closeness of Oneness, connecting back to the higher spiritual principle of "I am one with all."

On the opposite end of the spectrum, people who work with violet, create Spiritual systems and put order into those systems. They are inspiring and can be over-self sacrificing, and are dedicated, sometimes obsessed with, their cause.

The Chakra Color Energies

Energy manifests on Earth in Rays. The seven leptons that dance around the proton in each atom are those wondrous color energies. Remember which element to use and which body it corresponds to. The colors have to be attached to an Element. You can't have one without the other.

Pay attention to the vibration of each color energy. The frequency of vibration increases as we move up through the bodies. This is because as we move up, we can only do so through shedding matter, (our issues) causing our atoms to be farther and farther apart. There is more space between the atoms and molecules in each of the bodies, causing the color energies to be less intense(concentrated).

The closer the atoms are, the darker the color. The farther apart they are, the paler the color. When you are applying a color energy, you need to know what element and shade of color to apply to which body. For example, cornflower blue clouds for soul-mental, and corn flower blue water for astral.

Learn which Element to use. The five major elements associations with our bodies are:

- Earth - physical body
- Water - astral or emotional body
- Air - mental body
- Fire - soul body
- Ether - lower spirit planes and above

Electric colors are not to be used on human beings.
Sunlight will give an extra boost of energy when you need it.

Do not send these energies to other people without their permission. Learn to have good energy manners and other proper manners on the energy planes. Those manners are just as important in the unseen worlds as they are in the seen world.

Without becoming aware of, and deliberately developing good energy manners, including respect, you will not be allowed access to the Elemental Kingdoms, through whom all Mastery of anything is gained. The Elementals do not like bad manners in humans in particular. Women tend to learn good energy manners more quickly than men because they are taught many energy principles, seen and unseen, through the learning of containment of their energies because they are female.

Behave, respect, and learn the rules.

Sunlight contains seven basic visual energies, and two
that are at each end of the color spectrum, making nine.

- Infra red
- Red
- Orange
- Yellow
- Green
- Blue
- Indigo
- Violet
- Ultra violet

Wave lengths of colors were first measured in 1802. Now we have wavelengths, frequencies, and ultra violet and infrared frequencies, which are the color measures above and below our visible color spectrum. Electro-magnetic radiation (light) is responsible for the colors we see.

The seven major colors energies express the masculine force of radiance and separation in seven different ways. Each of the colors has a different influence on our physical, astral, mental and soul bodies. Each of the colors is associated with a particular chakra.

Manipulating the color energies can influence a person's mood. Our color preferences are clues to the working style of our mind. Response to color is emotional, primitive. "Don't let anyone try to make you mature!" she said, redly.

All forms of self expression works with the color energies, to promote the development of the individual with the intention of evolvement. We apply the color energies to evolve, which is assigned to the ascension theories in humankind.

The color energies support the long term healing of any illness in the body systems.

Too much or too long use of the color energies sensitizes you. You become too sensitive...too individuated. Too isolated...That's a sign to go rejoin the world.

The Seven Color Energies

Red

We begin with the root chakra, red, the slowest in vibration, and work our way up through the colors, on up through the violet crown chakra. The vibratory rate gets faster as we go up, and the wave length gets shorter.

On the PH scale, red is the most alkaline color, violet the most acid color. On a vibration scale, red is the slowest in vibration, violet the fastest.

- Red is one of the seven Major Color Energies
- Music note is C and it is located at the bottom tip of the spine
- Red helps with cold, wet conditions.
- Red works with the root chakra at the base of the spine.
- Red is the most magnetic, the slowest moving and the most alkaline of the color energies.
- Red is organic and earthy. Red works with the organic understanding of the self, the understanding of One.
- Red provides a sound physical body, good circulation, good digestion, and robust health.
- Red is a stimulant, pepping up the autonomic nervous system. When you see the color red, your pupils dilate, your blood pressure rises, and your pulse rate and hand tremors increase.
- Red corresponds to the endocrine system and works with the adrenals, kidneys, colon and bladder.
- Red helps with fast rebuilding in the physical body on a cellular level. If you need more strength, physically or emotionally, pull in red.
- Red is hot, stimulating, and alkaline.
- Vitality, stamina, and endurance are created when red is combined with the Earth element.

- The Red Personality has a need for physical contact, intense physical activity, and sensory gratification.
- Positive Red helps to develop compassion, forgiveness, gratitude, persistence, and a sense of goodwill.
- Red works with the energies of confrontation and courage.
- Red works with physical vitality and physical energy.
- Red works with the Will and Force energies that are attributed to leadership.
- Clear red works with purity and being real on the physical planes. It is associated with purity in the physical sense, as it is related to spirituality. True connection cannot take place without enough red on all levels, which means confrontation and connection of certain kinds have to take place.
- When you run out of energy and need it, have red around.
- People who work with red have stamina and endurance.
- Red supports individuality and insists on one committing to one's self.
- Red helps speed change.
- Red helps one to develop Resistance to disease
- An excess of red produces an excess of acid in the system.

A lack of red in the physical body can cause:
- abscesses
- anemia
- blood deficiencies
- low blood pressure
- boils
- poor circulation
- colds
- colic
- coma
- coughing
- fatigue
- fainting

- ¬ heart trouble
- ¬ hay fever

Too much red in the physical body can result in:
- ¬ headaches
- ¬ nosebleeds
- ¬ fevers
- ¬ nervousness
- ¬ vaginal infections
- ¬ hyperactivity
- ¬ over acidic conditions
- ¬ fever blisters
- ¬ any condition associated with heat

Emotionally, red helps to de-structure the victim role. If you don't have enough red, everything hurts your feelings. You can become paranoid. Red helps to physically create what is needed to protect your emotions. It gives presence and grounding. If you are going through a lot emotionally, if you pull in red, it will be like adding stamina and endurance to finish the job.

If your path was to deal with an over structured childhood, or if somebody browbeat you constantly, then the Individuation process was likely held up. This type of lifetime indicates a chronic lack of red on the higher energy planes, where "the "I am" and the "I will" of you develop their higher aspects. This lack of red can cause great stubbornness in the higher energy planes, along with a lack of stamina and a lack of ability to endure, that can sometimes show up as diarrhea or gas in the physical body.

Too much red on the emotional planes can manifests as hyperactivity or a fiery temper. (Note to Healers- Treat with blue and yellow after release of excess red.) To neutralize an excess of red, pull in or send blue immediately after working with red.

On the mental planes, positive red works with the forwarding of new ideas, tolerance, and good will.

There is a sense of goodwill, persistence, and the ability to be a logical thinker if red is mixed with yellow. Helps enhance telepathy, goodwill towards men, determination, criticism, and brotherly love.

Too much red on the mental planes can cause intolerance, resentfulness, sarcasm and touchiness.

Not enough red on the mental planes: you can't communicate or express your ideas, you rationalize everything, are argumentative, short tempered.

When red becomes negatively polarized on any of the planes of energy, the first thing the person does is become short sighted. Projection happens. Someone outside themselves did it to them. They may want to physically de-structure or destroy whatever they have blamed the problem on.

Red works with all metals and gemstones such as:
- Mineral is iron
- Garnet sand rubies
- copper and brass
- carnelian
- jasper
- some ambers
- bloodstone
- fire agate

Foods and minerals:
- zinc
- copper
- iron
- trace minerals
- magnesium
- potassium
- beets
- strawberries
- radishes

- ¬ apples
- ¬ plums
- ¬ tomatoes
- ¬ rhubarb

- ¬ Beef, a red meat, works with the color red and the Earth Element. It gives stamina and endurance. It is earth warrior food. People who don't eat red meat can get ungrounded very easily and become airy fairies.
- ¬ Red works best with square shapes.
- ¬ Red Earth is an excellent shield.
- ¬ Boring work to do? Find a room that's red and do it there.

Healers- use red with caution, because of the strength of the stimulation from this color, and the difficulty controlling it.

Orange

- ¬ Orange- is a Minor color energy that combines yellow from above, and red from below.
- ¬ Orange works with the second chakra.
  - o It is located 3-4 inches up from the base of the spine.
  - o The orange chakra magnetically spreads the Word to All. It disseminates the life energies, and is considered to be the seat of the life force in the Buddhist religions. Notice that they wear the color orange.
- ¬ Orange in the physical body turns into peach on the higher levels, as it becomes a combination of rose and yellow. In the physical world, peaches carry that same color, and are one of the foods that contain all seven color energies.
- ¬ Orange works with the higher expression of Wisdom.
- ¬ Orange works with the assimilation and distribution of other color energies, because it works with the Etheric principle of Unity. All is One.
- ¬ Orange works with the energy of Vitality.

- o Orange increases Vitality.
    - ♣ This chakra assimilates the Vitality from solar Prauna, the energy the sun gives off.
    - ♣ Orange is the color of vitality, it stimulates self expression, creativity, and "make it happen-ness".
- ¬ Orange works with the character development of true discrimination.
- ¬ Red stirs energy up, and orange makes it zing with vitality.
- ¬ Orange allows for the expression of magnetic or feminine joyousness in both men and women, and encourages us to risk expressing that joyousness.
- ¬ Orange is a sticky energy because it works with the Principle of Unity.
- ¬ Orange works with attachment.
- ¬ Spiritually, orange is the path of unity, sometimes at any cost.
- ¬ Orange works with sexuality. It is a warm energy that works with assimilation and the circulation processes.
- ¬ Orange encourages freedom from limitation, creative endeavors, increases enthusiasm, and raises joy.
- ¬ Orange raises your mentality, relieves Repression, helps induce tolerance, and strengthens the will.
- ¬ Orange works with the spleen's energy centers and vivifies and recharges the reproductive centers.
- ¬ Orange is a magnetic-color. Use it to stabilize almost any magnetic activity.
- ¬ Orange is a sticky, magnetic energy and a left-handed color.
    - o Orange is left handed while blue is right handed. They have opposite positive-negative positions. Blue's effect on the physical is magnetic-electro, while orange's effect on the physical is electro-magnetic.
    - o Blue is a projective color that works in a magnetic way

- Orange stimulates sexuality. People who work with orange emit a lot of sexual energy. Other people get either turned on by the sexual energies, or get irritated by them.
- On the lower energy levels, orange can turn into over attachment, resulting in a lack of discrimination about who to have sex with, how much sex to have, and possibly attaching to extremist religious groups and cults.

- Orange is organic. It works with organic Spirituality.
- On the Spirit planes, orange becomes gold and works with the principles of love and wisdom through desire.
- Orange helps one assimilate the truth.
- Orange stirs up the desire to connect.
- Too much orange on the soul planes can cause Spiritual insecurity, which sends you to one religion after another.
    - An extreme excess could even cause one to become an atheist.

- Positive orange on the soul planes–helps you attain spiritual security and stability.
- Allows pure love to filter down into the lower levels.
- Orange gives attention to the higher desires of the soul body to unite with All.
- Too much orange can cause intolerance, over indulgence.

- A good balance of orange in the physical helps over come fears. It makes you more secure, gives self assurance, freedom from limitation, gives energy to creative endeavors, helps keep mental balance and enlightenment, joy, proper assimilation and elimination.

Positive in physical body:
- Dries up mucus,
- provides freedom of action,
- relieves repression, discouragement and despondency

- helps overcome tendencies towards over self gratification.
- Orange removes mucous in the physical body, and helps stop crying and grief.
- Orange works with rejuvenation and regeneration in the pelvic region.

A lack of orange in the physical may cause:
- acidity
- anemia
- anger
- asthma
- blood ailments
- high blood pressure
- blood sugar difficulties
- bronchitis
- convulsions
- epilepsy
- female problems
- gall stones
- gout
- hemorrhoids
- hysteria
- menstrual instability
- mental instability
- rheumatism
- sexual imbalance
- phlegm
- nervous debility
- insanity
- insomnia
- kidney problems

- Positive Orange in the Emotional body helps transmute desires and raises your desire level. It sends energy to all the lower energy centers and encourages impulses of love and wisdom to generate.

¬ Positive Orange in the Mental body puts energy behind new ideas and creative endeavors- helps to produce and energize original and constructive ideas. Raises our mentality.

¬ Orange works with our intentions and the development of our faculties by creating a desire to learn and assimilate data.

¬ Orange works with:

¬ Shellfish of all kinds:
  o silver
  o nets
  o mesh
  o pearls
  o mother of pearl
  o the Moon

¬ In wild birds, the connective tissue holding bones and organs together is orange. The connective tissue of wild birds and most wild game is orange. This is one way you can eat orange and ground it to Earth.

¬ Orange works with
  o amber
  o abalone
  o carnelian
  o manganese
  o opalite
  o zinc
  o nickel
  o iron
  o coral
  o magnesium
  o oranges
  o tropical fruit juices
  o okra
  o olives
  o saffron
  o carrots

- o pumpkin
- ¬ The positive orange personality is humanitarian, competitive, hospitable, expansive, altruistic, optimistic, and warm.
- ¬ The negative orange personality is selfishly proud, superficial, mistrusting, power seeking, anti-social, social climbing and politically manipulative.
- ¬ Orange is the path of wisdom and love, united. The deeper needs are for social contact and acceptance in group and family, to have respect and a good reputation. Their biggest challenge is to learn to belong to the family of man through love and service, to make deeper contracts.
- ¬ Indigo and orange are combinations of colors, so they drop out in the physical plane, leaving 5 principal colors, which correspond to the laws of physical matter.
- ¬ The best shields to use are cloaking devices such as capes, glass jars and spiral staircases and seashells.
- ¬ Orange works with circles and triangles.
- ¬ Pink and orange mixed, gives a zest for life.
- ¬ Orange and violet ray people like to strut around on the astral elemental planes

Gold
- ¬ Use gold instead of orange for meditation.
- ¬ Gold has many similarities with orange, but comes from a higher energy plane, and is able to work with greater quantities and higher qualities of energy.
- ¬ Cadeus symbol-medicine-Kundalini health
- ¬ Works with golden fire up and down the sides of the spine.
- ¬ Gold has 79 protons and 79 electrons packed closely together inside each of its atoms, which causes it to give off its lovely golden sheen.

Yellow
- ¬ Yellow's music note is E
- ¬ Yellow-works with maintaining objectivity
- ¬ Yellow works with the solar plexus chakra- located just underneath the diaphragm in the physical body.
- ¬ Yellow is Electro-Magnetic.

- ¬ It is hard to ever have too much yellow. It is in the middle of the color spectrum along with blue and green.
- ¬ Pure, positive yellow (not electric yellow!) cleanses, illuminates, and inspires on all levels, and purifies.
- ¬ Yellow helps one to be decisive, discerning, and optimistic. Yellow produces a tonic effect on the nerves, and encourages mental activity.
- ¬ Yellow influences the high mind and the soul with objectivity's results.
- ¬ Yellow is associated with the planet Mercury.
- ¬ Yellow works with the skin and the lining of organs.
- ¬ Yellow works with the interior membranes.
- ¬ Yellow affects digestion at the solar plexus.
- ¬ Yellow soothes the nervous system.
- ¬ Yellow works with communication.
- ¬ Yellow inspires objectivity.
- ¬ Yellow stimulates our thought processes from an objective point of view.
- ¬ Yellow helps us learn more about ourselves. To have aha's.

Yellow on the astral planes:
- ¬ Too emotional? Draw in yellow to help the nervous system, so it can stabilize the alkaline-acid balance.
- ¬ Positive yellow in the astral or emotional body gives clarity.

¬ Yellow gives a sense of control over the emotions. A good balance of positive yellow emotionally, keeps us from projecting our emotions.

¬ Too much yellow on the astral planes causes one to be out of touch with their feelings.

¬ Yellow calms and helps the nervous system stay healthy.

¬ Yellow assists in clarifying the expression of higher desires.

¬ It assists in the clarity of, and the attunement of emotions through the re-establishing of centering.

¬ Yellow in the Mental body provides for clear ideas, understanding, wisdom and praise of God, stimulates higher mentality, and strengthens the mental body, the mental faculties, and clarity of thought.

¬ In combination with red, yellow assists in logic and reasoning, and stimulates production of the intellect.

¬ Enough yellow on the mental planes gives objectivity.

¬ Too much yellow on the mental planes causes one to be cold, impersonal and detached, and overly analytical. There is a loss of attachment to the emotions.

¬ Yellow gives the ability to articulate, it works with impersonal expression on the mental planes.

¬ Yellow on the soul planes:

¬ Yellow on the soul planes works with discernment, discrimination, and the ability to clearly see and understand what's going on. When we don't have enough yellow on the soul planes, we take universal principles too personally.

¬ Positive yellow:
  o Makes one logical, analytical, creative, flexible, eloquent, intensely self aware, methodical, expressive, precise, efficient in planning and organization.

¬ A good balance of positive yellow purifies the bodies, helps develop a healthy nervous system, decisiveness, gives the ability to comprehend easily and to be logical. Yellow can be used to help heal infections, and to counteract the effects of poison.

¬ Physical- cleanses the pores, purifies the bodily systems, helps develop the ability to get things done in an orderly fashion.

¬ Yellow works with the structure of the physical body. It Works with skin, eyes, bones, teeth, hair, finger nails, and the skeletal frame

¬ Not enough yellow in the physical body can manifest as a lack of vitamin C, dry skin, acne, seborrhea, eczema, other skin problems, bone loss, Alzheimer's.

¬ Dry skin is caused from excess yellow.

¬ Oily skin is not enough yellow.

- o Having enough yellow can help prevent problems with: acne
- o asthma
- o digestive problems
- o eczema
- o fever
- o flatulence
- o hay fever
- o heartburn
- o hysteria
- o impotence
- o indigestion
- o low blood sugar
- o lung ailments
- o nervous exhaustion
- o all skin conditions
- o tuberculosis
- o hair problems

- In the physical, excess yellow can cause fragile bones, a tendency to neglect the physical body, and nervous exhaustion.
  - It can make one impatient, overactive, and mentally intolerant. It can cause a situation where more information is accumulated than can be absorbed.

- Depressed? Use yellow for a lift.
- Yellow works with all kinds and colors of coral and ivory. Put coral and ivory in office to aid mental work. Brings mental clarity and cheerfulness.
- Brings clarity on the astral planes. Yellow allows for objectivity, the ability to be close, or to distance from a perspective, promotes understanding, and conceptual awareness. It brings objectivity on the mental planes.

- Negative yellow makes one
  - critical
  - nitpicky
  - contradictory
  - schizophrenic
  - verbose
  - egotistical
  - judgmental
  - separative
  - verbally aggressive
  - unable to feel
- If you want to learn about yourself, pull in yellow.
- Yellow helps retain emotional and mental objectivity.
- Therapists should use yellow to stay objective, to not get attached to clients' issues.
- Wearing or carrying a small piece of ivory will help balance men's feminine or magnetic nature.
- Wearing or carrying coral will help women to balance their masculine or electric nature.

- ¬ Yellow works with:
  - o calcium
  - o manganese
  - o potassium, phosphorous
  - o popcorn
  - o yellow squash
  - o lemons and citrus fruits
  - o Coral
  - o ivory
  - o silver
  - o aluminum
  - o nickel, platinum
  - o copper, gold
  - o shells
- ¬ Yellow has a cooling quality to it because it creates distance, which lessens friction on all the energy planes.
- ¬ People who work with yellow are very mental, analytical, and have a dry sense of humor and a good perspective. They are not particularly emotional, and they work well from objective observer positions.
- ¬ Yellow works with the path of Divine Intellect. The deepest needs are to live in an orderly world, to express a higher individuality, to shine intellectually, to understand.

Green

- ¬ Music note is F
- ¬ Green governs the Shields Brotherhood.
- ¬ Green governs all forms and kinds of shields.
- ¬ Green combines yellow from below and blue from above. The blue within green works to moderate the blood pressure, while the yellow stimulates the brain into more stable activity.
- ¬ Use an Army green, a mustard green, to make astral plane shields.
- ¬ Green Soothes jangled nerves. It is the path of balance. The deepest needs are to feel certain and secure, assertive and powerful, to love and be loved, to save up.

- ¬ Green works with the heart chakra which is located in the center of the chest in human beings.
- ¬ Green works with the heart center, circulation and organs.
- ¬ Green works with the thymus.
- ¬ Green works with being able to receive in the upper body.
- ¬ Green is the blanket healing color that is used for everything.
- ¬ Green works with balance in all areas.
- ¬ Green works with the cardiovascular system and with all facets of proper circulation.
- ¬ Green works with organs and blood
- ¬ Green is the physical antibiotic.
- ¬ For any emergency, grab green first.
- ¬ Green is neither acid or alkaline.
- ¬ Green promotes growth and harmony.
- ¬ Green oils the joints.
- ¬ On planet Earth, green equals harmony through conflict.
- ¬ Green promotes the ability to laugh at one's self.
- ¬ There are lots of ways to get green on this planet. There are lots of greens and vegetables here.

- ¬ In the physical body, green gives strength.
- ¬ Green creates balance, and neutralizes inharmonious vibrations within the aura.
- ¬ Green helps one become attuned to the universal energy supply.
- ¬ Green in the emotional body soothes the nervous system, balances desires, helps one to see reality more clearly on the desire level, enables one to develop a non-critical sense of brotherliness, counteracts jealousy, and works with the ability to give and receive connection.
- ¬ Green balances the feminine-masculine, magnetic and electric energies, through the emotions.
- ¬ Too little green on the astral planes creates extreme psychological dependencies, the need to hold on to something outside of yourself to stay balanced.

- A lack of green emotionally can also cause a scattering of energy, nervousness, lack of feeling safe, and emotional wobbles that manifest in fear
¬ Green in the mental body promotes the balanced growth of the mental body, along with purity of self.
¬ Green helps one to develop a sense of humor and detached sympathy. Green on the mental planes gives a lively sense of humor.
¬ A lack of Green on the mental planes causes one to tell lies.
¬ Mentally, a lack of green can cause excessive worry, anxiety, and panic attacks.
¬ A lack of green in the physical can cause:
    - boils
    - venereal diseases
    - blood pressure problems
    - excess acidity
    - nose bleeds
    - heart murmurs
    - heart attacks
    - swelling
    - neuralgia
    - nervous disorders
    - throat problems
¬ An excess of green can cause one to try to accomplish too many things at one time. To be hyperactive.
¬ A good balance of green produces a sense of well being on all levels. A feeling of stability. Helps one to relax and overcome anxiety, irritability, and intolerance. It promotes rapid healing and helps rebuild health after illness.
¬ On the soul planes, green promotes not taking one's self too seriously. It helps the self bring about and maintain balance and stability on all the energy planes.
¬ Green is not neutral. Green space is neutral.
¬ It is the creative color.
¬ Even though it is hard to get too much green, it happens. Consider using alternating colors on long term projects.

¬ Green assists in sacro-cranial rebalancing.

¬ Positive green causes one to be:
  o generous
  o vital
  o powerful
  o secure
  o open hearted
  o nurturing
  o self-assertive
  o compassionate
  o expansive

¬ People who work with green are physically healthy. They have very sensitive feelings. They wear their hearts on their sleeves.

¬ People who work with green take all relationships as personal.

¬ The green personality stirs up imbalance in order to grow and not be bored. People who work with green are multi-talented, very creative, and have many things going on at the same time. Musicians, artists and writers most always work with green on a personality level.

¬ On the astral planes, those who have too much green demand too much attention.

Guilt is also related to green. It is an excess or lack thereof, creating a chronic imbalance of green.

¬ Negative green can cause one to be:
  o miserly
  o depleted
  o doubting
  o insecure
  o jealous
  o possessive
  o selfish

- o attached
- o envious
- o mistrustful

¬ Green works with malachite,
- o emeralds,
- o peridot,
- o copper,
- o green vegetables and many other things on planet Earth.

¬ A balance of green on the higher mental and soul planes gives the knowledge to heal.

¬ Green is especially useful for shock.
- o For Shock in physical- use blue
- o Shock emotionally- astral- use green
- o Shock –mental –use red
- o Shock in the soul- use indigo or violet
- o Astral- green works with the ability to give and receive connection.

¬ Use green or blue water for cuts.

¬ The use of green will help heal burns, and counteracts the effects of poison and Possession.

¬ Green is the color of connection because it sits exactly in the middle -center of the color spectrum.

¬ For any emergency-use a green cloud image.

¬ Cut or bleeding- bring green water past knees

¬ Use blue for astral anxiety, green for mental anxiety.

Blue

¬ Music note is G and it is located in the throat area.

¬ Green works with the organs and the blood. Blue works with everything else.

¬ Blue soothes jangled nerves. It is the path of the detailed mind. The deepest needs are to have inner peace, to find mental security, to live out an ideal.

¬ To be heard, use blue.

- Blue is the tranquilizer energy that is to be used on all levels and in all bodies.
- Blue is an electro-magnetic energy. Blue is cooling and slimming.
- Blue works with creativity, enlightenment, expression of higher truths, and with the throat in the physical body.
- Blue helps you become diplomatic, reliable, resourceful, and stable. This is the color that enables philosophers and others to express themselves well with words.
- Blue works with the throat chakra.
- Blue in the physical body is the color used for everything. Nervousness, stings, bites, cuts, breathing disorders, throat problems, muscle problems, ear, eye and nose problems.
- Blue is the most magnetic of all the colors from a projective point of view.
- Blue expedites tranquility and calm throughout the physical, emotional, mental, and soul bodies. It smoothes and soothes and mellows.
- Use turquoise on the emotional planes for protection and aqua-watery blues to calm the brain and nervous system. Emotionally- used for relaxation and astral traveling.
- Use sky blues on the mental planes to calm the brain and nervous system.
- Use cornflower or royal blue to calm the mind down on the soul planes. Pay attention to the fact that the blue color gets lighter and softer as it travels up through the bodies.

- On the mental planes, blue bestows the capacity to clearly see the truth.
    - Blue confronts with truth without judgment.
- Blue encourages constant flexibility on the soul planes.
- Use soft cornflower blue for shock on the soul planes.
- On the soul levels, blue works with understanding truth and relaxation about the truth.

- Blue is a tranquilizer energy that is to be used in all bodies.
- Losing it? Panicked? Use blue and green.
- Every communication, every release of energy, all sounds from the self, forms of expression, occurs through blue.
- A lack of blue in the physical may cause:
    o laryngitis,
    o abscesses,
    o bleeding,
    o inflamed bowels,
    o prostrate trouble,
    o bleeding gums,
    o lung problems.
- All heat related issues are a lack of blue.
- An excess of blue causes one to become
    o egotistical,
    o very self centered,
    o tendency to become over irritated.
- An excess of blue can cause thinness.
- A good balance of blue enables one to stay calm, with clear thought processes, and to be emotionally balanced and optimistic. One becomes electro-magnetic much more easily. One also emits healing and soothing energies to others in their presence.
- Blue promotes rapid healing of burns, cuts, hiccups, pain, and lungs.
- Dizziness is a lack of blue.
- Blue works with sheaths and all coatings in the physical body. All nerve endings are covered with blue sheaths.

- Positive blue in the physical enhances your love of beauty, allows you to be of service to others, to be tactful, and the ability to comprehend and apply new ideas more quickly than most people.

- On the astral planes, positive blue soothes and supplies psychic energies to the astral body. Blue always works with the controlling of psychic forces. Psychic forces always come from separation or connection. Blue has to be present if the psychic forces are coming from connection.

- Negative blue on the astral planes causes one to be dull, lazy, and distrustful of other people.

- One of the negative aspects of working with blue, is that one can fall into the stance that neither they nor anyone else is quite good enough. It could have been done better, or more perfectly.
- Lack of blue on the emotional planes causes irritation, quick temper, depression, withdrawal.

- Blue on the Mental planes provides one with the ability to comprehend truth easily and to verbally express it well.
- Blue enables the higher mind to project ideas which expand the intellect. It allows appreciation of the mathematical beauty of form, and brings inspiration.

- Blue in the soul planes give access to higher truths and the ability to share high truths with others.

- Blue helps one to have a love of nature, and the ability to express and fulfill one's higher desires.

- Blue works with understanding the truth and relaxing about it on the soul planes. What will be, will be.

- On the soul planes, people who work with blue are able to heal others through expression of higher truths.

- If you are working with preparation for connection with another person, use blue.
- If you are terrified or extremely contracted any place, use blue, then green to eliminate fear and worry.

People who work with blue are very quiet and observant. They are the nit pickers, detail oriented, order experts. These people get more done without it looking like they are working, than anybody else. They are efficient and effective. Most of them have beautiful skin. They have a great love of beauty, are tactful, and are in service to others. They are able to pick up and apply new ideas quicker than average.

- Tense? Move into a blue room in imagination or in the physical.

- Blue works with:
  - zinc
  - nickel
  - copper
  - blueberries
  - all diamond shapes
  - honeycomb symbols
  - opals
  - moonstones
  - all the b vitamins
  - blue banded agate
  - blue lace agate
  - chalcedony
  - sodalite
  - turquoise
  - quartz
  - aquamarine
  - labradorite
- Use blue with topaz because topaz gemstones put power behind all other gems.

- For healers, know that the water element and sky is blue's natural home of disbursement.

- The positive blue personality can be:
  - content,
  - idealistic,

- o patient,
- o enduring,
- o nostalgic,
- o committed,
- o devotional,
- o peaceful,
- o synthesizing,
- o authoritative
- o loyal

¬ The negative blue personality can be:
  - o smug
  - o self-satisfied
  - o dogmatic
  - o resistant to change
  - o melancholic
  - o fanatic
  - o authority seeking
  - o rigid
  - o authoritarian
  - o ultra conservative
  - o slow to respond

Indigo

¬ This is the third eye energy located in the center of the forehead. The early indigo people are the Paul Reveres announcing the changes that are coming through naming the Masters and organizing their work.

¬ They are associated with the energies of the star systems and they are old souls.

¬ They work to anchor and raise the energies.

¬ They tend to try to please others by accommodating their lesser energies.

¬ Music note is A

¬ Indigo is composed of violet from above, and green and blue from below.

- Indigo is the path of devotion without skepticism. The deepest needs are to feel at one with the universe, to have conflict free relationships, to invent spiritually related improvements.
- Indigo is a fast-moving short-wave energy, commonly used in sacred rituals because it works with the higher planes of energy.
- Indigo works with transmutation of low energies into higher, more positive energies. It does this through the development of insights. All insights are indigo. Insight of all kinds is dependent on the proper functioning of the brow chakra.
- Indigo people need to learn to hold energy steady for the new people coming in. They are learning how to embody their Light without lowering their vibrations to match the conscious collective on Earth.
- They have to learn to not go off on yet another spiritual journey.
- They hold the imprints of all of their past lives and can readily correlate those memories to the collective.
- They are here to lighten the burden by transforming consciousness through a process involving changing carbon-based DNA into a more crystalline DNA with a higher vibration which causes more space between atoms which causes more light to be in the Being, and the result is that one becomes more like the universe than before, therefore reaping more understanding of the universe and how it operates. This is a universal inclusion process.
- Indigo is electro- magnetic.
- Indigo purifies the blood stream and mental processes.
- Indigo promotes clear and logical thoughts.
- Indigo helps one to develop tolerance, clarity of perception, and encourages one to seek enlightenment and At-one-ment.

Indigo works with the third eye chakra. When you open the third eye energy center, you can see and understand life as it actually exists. You can see both the positive and the negative and it both makes you happy and is painful. This takes many lifetimes.
Indigo combines power with practicality.

- ¬ Indigo can induce local anesthesia, and in some cases, total anesthesia.
- ¬ Indigo is used to heal mental and emotional instability, clinical schizophrenia, and nerve stability.
- ¬ Indigo stabilizes through assimilation of energies. It pulls in the higher energies of balance to work with the lower energies of harm and chaos.
- ¬ Indigo corresponds to the spleen chakra.
- ¬ Indigo works with the endocrine system, the eyes, the sinus and the sinus cavities, the pineal and thyroid, and pituitary glands.
- ¬ The master glands in the body for the entire chemistry of the body are behind the eyes.
- ¬ Indigo works with the whole big picture. Indigo works with the re-establishment of balance of the overall picture to regain the correct spiritual context.
- ¬ Emotional and mental instability, or one might call them mental or emotional illness, is a lack of indigo.
- ¬ Indigo is the color that instantly speeds up the movement of molecules in space. Indigo is to be used in emotional, mental, soul and spiritual imbalances as its rate of vibration is so high.

- ¬ Indigo air works with breaking out of one's own habit attachment. If you are trying to get over yourself, it breaks the hold of the investment you have, whatever it is. This is valuable when trying to release addiction patterns.

- ¬ For bad drug runs, (legal or otherwise), work with indigo to re-establish the balance between the emotional and mental bodies through the third eye, which blows open when someone is doing drugs, causing too much energy to pour through the system.

The same goes for opening the third eye too quickly. This causes problems to the meridian structures in all the other bodies and take years to repair. Know this before you decide that you have to "see" more. Because you will by law, have to process the both the positive and negative of the new things you are "seeing". You can't have one without the other.

- ¬ One of Indigos deepest needs is to have a conflict free relationship.

- ¬ Indigo helps to develop trust within you that others can rely on.

- ¬ For high fevers in the physical body, when children or anyone is having nightmares and seeing bad things, put them in water or put water on them because it is magnetic and cooling and will help them reconnect.
- ¬ Use indigo for any form of convulsion or epilepsy.

- ¬ If you get too much indigo, it will split into green, blue, and violet.
- ¬ Indigo works with clear logical thought, purifying of the bloodstream, and mental purifying. It combines the deep blue of devotion with a stabilizing red tone.

- ¬ Excess indigo may cause lack of control over one's faculties, mental confusion and numbness, and a tendency to become intolerant, irritable, and temperamental in a hysterical way.

- ¬ A good balance of indigo helps to counteract obesity.
- ¬ Indigo acts as a purifying agent on all levels.
- ¬ Indigo helps one to develop clear perception.
- ¬ Indigo helps one attain a sense of unity on all levels.

- In the physical body, indigo:
  - purifies the bloodstream,
  - nourishes tissues,
  - improves complexion,
  - strengthens the body
  - assists in the control of the higher bodies.

- In the emotional body indigo works with:
  - eye, ear and nose problems,
  - sinus and their cavities,
  - asthma,
  - bronchitis,
  - pneumonia,
  - paralysis,
  - delirium,
  - obsession,
  - insanity
  - possession.

- In the mental body indigo:
  - acts as a mental freeing and purifying agent.
  - you to develop a sense of unity
  - Helps develop self knowledge, and a well-developed mental body
  - Enables you to share and teach others
- On the soul planes, indigo helps you to develop the higher senses of sight, hearing, and smell.

- Indigo enables you to express the purity of your god self on the Spirit planes of energy that lie past the soul body. From this, you can learn to be a true spiritual teacher who can impart to others high knowledge, understanding, love, and wisdom. To refine the super senses.

- Indigo helps you to learn control of your universe through the five outer chakras, with the goal of achieving Spiritual consciousness. To feel at one with the universe.

¬ Too much indigo can cause mental confusion, and make one numb on the mental planes. This happens because too much indigo can act as an anesthesia to the mental body. This includes a lack of control of faculties.

¬ Indigo, when in balance, gives clear perception and a sense of union.

¬ Indigo works with:
- iron
- copper,
- diamonds,
- onions,
- lapis lazuli,
- eggplant,
- alexandrite,
- labradorite
- spectrolite.

♣ On a personality level, the indigo people are:
  - teachers
  - spiritual helpers
  - shamans
  - doctors
  - nurses
    ♣ They have to attend to the higher order of union, the control of the higher bodies, and learn how that takes place.
    ♣ They are learning psychic responsibility.
    ♣ They like structures that are ceremonial and many of them help others define rituals, both sacred and mundane.
    ♣ They have the ability to understand others on an emotional level, to

sympathize with others while sticking to their own path.

- ♣ They know where they are going, what they want to accomplish, and must.
- ♣ They have a larger sense of unity, and an ability to share on all levels.

¬ They are teachers of higher knowledge, wisdom and love.
¬ They work with control of psychic forces through ritual and ceremony.

¬ Positive indigo makes them:
- o supersensitive,
- o visionary,
- o far seeing,
- o to have aesthetic abilities, and
- o to be abstract,
- o inspired,
- o telepathic,
- o trusting of the future, and able to tune into the inner worlds of others.

¬ Negative indigo can cause these people to be:
- o inefficient
- o unable to live in the now
- o forgetful
- o fearful of the future
- o spaced out
- o undisciplined
- o introverted
- o always late
- o misguidedly futuristic
- o unable to manifest

¬ Indigo people are the visionaries of the future.

Violet

- ¬ Music note is B and it is the crown chakra energy
- ¬ Violet is composed of red from below and blue from above.
- ¬ Violet works with the crown chakra.
  - o The crown chakra works with the whole spinal column.
- ¬ The deepest needs are to bring order out of chaos, to have sympathy and tenderness, to have constant communication with the universe and to remove time from its limiting structures.

- ¬ It is the fastest moving, highest in vibration of the color energies, and has the shortest wave length.
- ¬ It is the most electric color, the most stringent, fast moving color, therefore it is highly stimulating.
- ¬ Like indigo and red, this is another color to use with great caution.
- ¬ On all energy levels violet helps to develop higher understanding, intuition, and knowing.
- ¬ It enables one to eventually achieve God consciousness, then one can help others follow their spirit path.
- ¬ Violet is more electric than magnetic. However, it does work with magnetic energies to some extent. It possesses an intense electro-chemical power, and is the ideal purifier.
- ¬ It blends the love and will attributes of the color red with the truth and devotion attributes of the color blue, and combined, they encourage you to work to achieve the highest of divine ideals.
- ¬ Violet inspires one to their personal God-ness.
- ¬ In the physical body, violet provides nourishment to the upper brain and the sensory organs.
- ¬ It gives one a great appreciation of color and works of art.
- ¬ Violet works with purification and transmutation.
- ¬ Violet corresponds to the kidneys and works with kidney problems.
- ¬ Violet works with the kidneys elimination system.

¬ Violet in the emotional body stirs up the nervous system and helps transmute one's lower desires into higher desires.

¬ Violet assists with the meditation process by stilling the emotional body.

¬ Emotionally, violet is used for purification and stimulation.

¬ Mentally, violet transmutes negative thoughts and works with the sub conscious to See.

¬ Violet teaches higher truths. On the soul planes, violet is the energy of tradition, order and form, morals, rules, and codes of ethics.

¬ Violet is the Brotherhood of rituals, occult wisdom, and ceremonial magic, which gives one the methodology to accomplish what one needs to. How to do it. How to be who you are.

¬ Violet works with the transmutation of desires, and the development of self esteem.

¬ Negatively, people who work with violet may have to deal with having too much self importance, fanaticism, or being one who has a constant insistence on having a too narrow view of the world or others, or a need for perfection that can never be achieved.

¬ An excess of violet can make one:
   o highly nervous
   o intolerant
   o irritable
   o confused
   o depressed
   o or irrational

¬ A lack of violet can cause:
   o backaches,
   o baldness,
   o bladder problems,
   o nervous and mental disorders,
   o scalp problems,

- o epilepsy,
- o tumors
- o leukemia.
¬ Violet in balance activates one's intuition and inspirational energies on all levels.
  - o It encourages dedication to the higher ideals you have.
  - o It pushes you to attain high truths.

  - o Violet in the mental body:
  - o expands your mental horizons
  - o builds and nourishes the mental body
  - o stimulates the desire to achieve higher understanding
  - o purifies ideals

¬ Positive violet people are
  - o creative,
  - o charming
  - o possess a sense of wonder
  - o They have a mystical instinct for divine order
  - o They carry the power of transformation.

¬ Negative violet people have a negative self image, are day dreamers, and sharply critical.

¬ Violet helps heal stings.
¬ Violet counteracts the effects of Possession.
¬ Violet helps with neurosis.
¬ Violet creates a lot of heat when used.
¬ Violet works with:
  - o amethyst
  - o labradorite
  - o spectrolite
  - o iron
  - o platinum
  - o grapes
  - o wine

- o blackberries,
- o cordials, eggplant
- o elderberries

¬ Do not use violet except very briefly!
¬ People who work with violet typically talk a lot about the past.
¬ They are historians with a lot of information at their disposal. They are into the ceremonial aspects of life.
¬ They love rich clothing, pomp and circumstance.
¬ Points of view are most important to them. (Like Andy Rooney)
¬ Negatively, they can become obsessed with details of the past.
¬ They can live in the past and not be present for their current life. They jump from the tiniest detail to an impossibly large view of the world, in which they love everybody, but it's never effective.
¬ Their deepest need is to bring order out of chaos, to be surrounded with sympathy and tenderness, and to have an eternal communion with the universe going on to achieve the annihilation of time.

Extra Notes on the Color Energies:

ᛒ Red and violet are at opposite ends of the color spectrum. For all healing purposes, use the mid range colors of green, blue and yellow for safest results.

ᛒ The most masculine color is the most electric-violet. It is the least magnetic, and is used very cautiously in healing processes.

ᛒ Indigo is the next most masculine color, and must be used very sparingly.

ᛒ Indigo and violet have very different and specific effects and both are very strong.

ᛒ Blue is used to stabilize any electric activity.

ᛒ Green is in the middle therefore, it is electro-magnetic-and balanced.

ᛒ Yellow soothes, orange stimulates in a magnetic way, and then red, which is the most magnetic, therefore almost never applied.

¬ For Shock in physical - use blue
¬ For emotional shock - use green
¬ For shock in mental - use red
¬ For shock in Soul - use indigo or violet

ᛒ Always use the appropriate element with the colors.
ᛒ Color energies work with the acid balance in the physical body.
    o Too much Color energy causes diarrhea.
    o Too much of the Elements can cause constipation. That's how you know when you have too much of one or the other.

ϖ Use yellow, blue and green for general healing and if you don't know what to use, because they are in the middle of the color spectrum.

ϖ The ends of the color spectrum are to be used only in specific healing circumstances. They are used for specific time limits and only in specific areas.

ϖ Always state "This is being done in the highest good of All."

ϖ Learn how to send and release energy.

ϖ Use good energy manners. Without them, you won't get very far and you may get yourself in trouble.

ϖ Learn to release the Excess Energies, stating that they are to be used in the highest karmic good.

ϖ Use stained glass windows or theater lights to bring colors to others. Don't use combinations of sounds and colors from synthesizers. Synthesizers do not work for healing.

ϖ A medium to darker Green is to be used in all emergency situations to bring balance. It's in the middle of the color spectrum and associated with the heart chakra. Too much green breaks down into blue and yellow, so it is safest to use.

Here are some techniques and methods that other Color Healers have invented down through time.

A brief history of Color Healers

Here are a few highlights. There are many more. Just search them out, and learn their techniques and intentions.

6th. Century B.C. Orpheus applied vibrational medicine of color and light as a means of healing and promoting spiritual awareness. Both Pythagoras and Plato were influenced by his teachings.
Color rooms were used as sanctuaries for healing in ancient China, Egypt and India.

Ayurvedic is an ancient healing practice that goes back thousands of years. In this system, there are five Elements, Earth, Water, Air, Fire and Ether, and their associated Colors. Each individual has their specific amounts of these energies comprising their personality and constitution. The Elemental balance is restored through working with the color energies. So the idea of alternative healing has been around a long time.

125 A.D.-Apuleius experimented with the flickering light to Determine epilepsy.

200- Ptolemy observed that sun light coming into people's eyes made them feel happy.
17th. Century- Pierre Janet used flickering light to reduce hysteria in hospital patients.

In modern times, Isaac Newton divided the light down into the color energies.

Johann Wolfgang Goethe studied the psychological effect of the color energies on human beings.

1851- Jacob Lorber wrote about the healing powers of sunlight when used to heal the soul and to cross over into a better world.

This is associated in later times with the spiritual nature of near death experiences.

1876 - Augustus Pleasanton stimulated the glandular system with blue light.
In the same year, *Seth Pancoast* stimulated the nervous system with red light. (The glandular system works slower than the nervous system)

1877 - Neils Finson began Modern color therapy.

1878 - Dr. Edwin Babbitt experimented with water and sunlight to treat a variety of ailments, including burns, nervous excitability, and cold in the extremities.

1897- Dinshah Ghadiali M.D. shined indigo light onto a patient's body and saved her life. He advanced color phototherapy, and assigned the specific attributes of the colors to the behavioral attributes of physiology. He made correspondences between minerals and colors. He made formulas to apply colors directly to the body to influence healing. He developed a system of healing using all the colors of the spectrum, plus purple, magenta, and scarlet. His book is titled "The Triumph of Spectrachrome".

The Dinshah Health Society was formed in 1975, and still exists.

1908 - Aura Soma was developed in England. It used colors to heal physical and emotional symptoms and promote psychological change.

1926- C. G. Sanders specified that application of particular colors is necessary for normal health.

1930 "The Father of Spectro Chrome Metry" *Dinshah Ghadiali M.D.,* compiled an encyclopedia of treatment using color and light to treat over 400 hundred ailments.

1932 - Gerrard and Hessay, two California psychologists scientifically established some of the effects of the light spectrum.

1941 - Harry Riley Spitler, M.D., formulated the Syntonic principle, which states that light coming through the eyes balances the autonomic nervous system.

1991 - Harrah Conforth, M.D., color and light applied to encourage whole brain synchronization. *Robert Cosgrove M.D.* used colored light for sedative properties before, during, and after surgeries.

Because Light can harm as well as heal, be very careful.

A few of the spiritual results of working with the color energies:

- ¬ We gain more awareness of the environment we live in.
- ¬ We become able to see parts of life we were not aware of.
- ¬ We improve our responses to other people's emotions and thinking.
- ¬ We begin a structured, orderly process to further develop our psychic and mental telepathy skills.
- ¬ The color energies help us build channels for our intuition.
- ¬ Working with the color energies gives more life, action and spirit to the chakras, and results in them opening more in each of our bodies.
- ¬ Increases the stored energy we use to enlarge our conscious awareness, resulting in more spiritual awakenings.
- ¬ Opening of the Chakras

The Mystic Marriage and the Higher Chakras

Buddha and Jesus were both Elemental Masters and higher Spiritual scientists. Buddha's top knot and Jesus's halo are symbols of a completely opened crown chakra. That happens when all of the chakras are open. This signifies ownership of a fully developed Cosmic brain. No one reaches enlightenment without understanding the Cosmos they are a part of. This is the significance of developing a Cosmic brain. This comes about through what is called the Mystic Marriage.

The Higher Chakras

Most metaphysical teachings tell us we have seven major chakras throughout our bodies. Some studies list both minor and major chakras and elsewhere.

But, we also have chakras outside of our bodies that are connected to us. Those chakras constantly connect and remind our individual life force what the universe means to us, and reminds us that we are a part of the universe, and are connected to it at all times. Those chakras define our place in the larger scheme of Life.

We live and die just as the stars in the cosmos do. To track the birth and magnificent death of a star, is to track our own beginning and endings.
We are a particle connected to and moving within a larger universe. Everything we know about is participating in the larger universal laws. Our connection to All of Life is maintained through the vital Cosmic energies, the collection of Universal, Galactic Super cluster, Solar system, Sun, And Planetary Energies that run through the personal chakra system connected to the Etheric web located outside of our bodies. We must be fed these energies in order to maintain being a part of the cosmos. To exist. It is the Larger Law of All.

This happens through the chakra system. The Cosmic collection of these five energies, and probably others, are fed to our Etheric web through the outer chakras that gravitate outside of, and around our head and bodies. These chakras are energetically aligned with the ridges in the upper occipital lobe of the head, and are attached at strategic areas to the Etheric body, and to the causal bodies of each part of manifested collective matter on this planet. That includes human beings.

The Etheric body works with the Ether Element. It looks like a net or web surrounding ourselves. No one knows exactly how far out it is from our bodies, but we can estimate that it is fluid, flexible, and at places, within a few inches of our physical body. The vibration of the Etheric web resonates to the grids surrounding Earth and is a match for them therefore, causing healing to our bodies to be available through the Colors and Elements that comprise Earth. The magnetic energy grids surrounding Earth - its Etheric web.

Each one of the Cosmic energy chakras works with a different part of the Etheric body, the energy body, the web or net that surrounds us.

What causes our Cosmic chakras to spin at a higher vibration?
All the outer chakras spin at a higher vibration, and this is why. The Etheric body resides where it outside of self, so it has very little matter to slow the spin down. It is fluidic and delicate as a result, but extremely strong.
When the Etheric body is rent or torn or damaged in some way, it takes spiritual energy to get to it and do the work to heal it. You can't get there to heal it or even work on it, until the energy is high enough in vibration. This is why rituals and spiritual ceremonies have to be the tools used to pave the way to Etheric body healing. Imagination must be used, too.

Here is how: Think of the Etheric Web as a web or a grid, with crossing points.
At each crossing point is seated a spinning sphere containing and maintaining a small amount of the perfect, most delicately tuned,

chemical mix of colors and elements, just suited for you, that came from the universe birthing a star somewhere a long time ago. Billions of years ago.

These delicate, perfectly and personally balanced chakra systems, feed constantly measured doses of the Cosmic energies to each particle of us, so that we are maintained in the deeper understanding of the Greater Forces we are a tiny part of. These chakras connect us to our Cosmic Elders who reside in the Great Cosmic Seas, and elsewhere.

We have a built-in tracker so the universe knows where we are at all times. Under the third eye sits a hologram of the earth at the bridge of the nose in human beings. This seats the third eye into Earth's dimensions, and grounds it there. It is our identity map that allows the cosmic chakras to attach to, and work with the Earth dimensions. This hologram also identifies us as to where we are located in this universe.

The cosmic chakras are connected to the upper occipital ridge in the head, and from there, their energies are transported faster than the speed of light, which means other time dimensions, into portals running from your cranial plates and out to about 18 inches around your face, like a mask of energy.

Your sense of smell and sight is faster than any of your other senses. These are the senses that regulate the speed of, and send these energies into the rest of the system.

We stay connected to the cosmos through the intervention of these outer chakras. The Universe is 13.8 billion years old. The Earth is 4 and a half billion years old.

These chakras spin faster than the seven physical body chakras. That is why they reside outside of the physical body. They have to reside outside of the body because of their higher vibration. They spin faster, in order to maintain the linkage between us and the universal energies. These chakras embody and maintain for each of us, the Law that All Life lives by, so that All can continue to exist.

These chakras are faster moving than our physical, mental, astral, and soul bodies. That means that we have a permanent connection to the cosmos that lasts after we transcend our physical bodies.

To study the Cosmos is to learn how higher beginnings and endings happen and how true separation and true connection works. This study allows further membership into the larger understanding of the higher, collective, spiritual Nature of Life. From this, we understand more of how we are alike. This kind of work helps the opening of the higher inner chakras. We are truly Star material.

We go through the same birth, aging and death process the stars go through. We do this to refine and collect the best of ourselves for our next adventure in the cosmos, just as the stars do.

Now, on to the Mystic Marriage process. This process takes place over all of your lifetimes, so don't get in a hurry.

The halo and topknot are the feminine aspect of divine wisdom having been achieved.

Wisdom is derived from the word wise. This has everything to do with those outer chakras.

Binah is one of the 12 chakras named in the Kaballah. It is the solar plexus chakra and is attached to the astral body of mankind. The Chokmah is the third eye chakra and is attached to the mental body of mankind.

- ¬ All character development is developed through the feminine nature. It takes the lead.
- ¬ The mental body is governed through the air element.
- ¬ The astral body is governed through the water element.
- ¬ The mental body has a masculine polarity.
- ¬ The astral body has a feminine polarity.

63

This is the air and water element working together, the mind developing conscious structures for the emotions, the water element, to pour into.

When the feeling and thinking nature of a person becomes developed enough to interact, a process of divine character development begins at that time.

The solar plexus and third eye chakras interact together to develop divine wisdom. Informed wisdom. As the energies arc back and forth between these two centers, the heart chakra is activated into understanding love in a larger, wiser way.

Wisdom is created from the interaction between the mental body the chakma is attached to, and the feeling and intuitive nature, which the astral body is attached to, and love is no longer left to roam about and get in trouble as it pleases. It is now monitored and directed. We call this being wise, having wisdom. Some people like it, some don't.

Both the female astral body and the male nature of the mental body are now working as a team, and the psychic circuits of intuition and sight are activated. They are called upon to look for the divine wisdom in all situations from then on. They have moved into a position that provides for a certain kind of divine stability. That's when you know the truth and will take a stand for it, regardless of the cost.

The solar plexus and the third eye interact. The third eye being the masculine center of sight, and the solar plexus being the center of intuition and the contact point for the feeling nature.

This is a development of the divine feminine aspect. No character development takes place without the Elemental Kingdoms overseeing it. The old owl symbolizes the aspect of midnight, the most feminine time of the day for the third eye.

Overseeing this Elemental process in humanity is the Archangel Tzaphkiel who rules over the Ophanim angels who are the carriers of the throne of God, and who are said to be great wheels covered with eyes, hence, the third eye.

As these two chakras learn to work together, an energy path is created, and the heart opens into a new understanding of Divinity, and the crown charka lifts and a halo is created. Budda's topknot and the halo of Jesus are symbols of this degree of Divine discernment having been achieved through the blending of the color and elemental energies.

This is a Divine feminine position in the development of character in the realms of becoming an Elemental master of a particular rank. Both the Christ and Budda were higher Elemental Masters.
Out of this process comes:
- Modesty
- Perfection
- Innocence
- Gentleness
- Meekness
- Kindness
- Yielding
- Merciful
- Goodwill
- Help

One of the wisdoms that come out of this is that Race is not a concept of separation, rather, it is a concept and process of individuation.

When this energy begins to activate, one must repent and rectify all flaws, thus creating new divine character development.
Here is how it works.

The Etheric body is not an aura. Auras are the energy emanations exuding from the electric and magnetic fluids in all of the bodies. Everything that is living in this physical world has an etheric double that corresponds to changes in the physical body. The connection to the Etheric body is served through the changes that occur in the endocrine system in humans.

The emotional energies ride the endocrine system.

We are constantly processing energy through our chakras. Twenty four hours a day, every instant of our life. The nervous system processes the faster, automatic energies such as breathing and body movement.

The endocrine system works with the nervous system and processes the slower energies. It is made up of glands, and governs the secretion of hormones.

The energy received into each chakra carries its own vibratory range. Energy comes in and we experience Life. Then it is sent back out to the chakra network to be expressed. The sets of chakras correspond in vibration to each of the energy bodies.

The slowest moving energy comes in at the base, or root, chakra. The energy range streaming into the solar plexus chakra is received by the emotional Nature, which rides the endocrine system. Our sub-conscious programming resides in this chakra. The patterning for how we process energy comes from our parents, from birth to puberty, and is received through the solar plexus.

The energy comes in, and mother and father's energy separates. Father's energy goes to the liver meridian overlay. Mother's energy goes into the kidney and spleen overlay.

We experience and assimilate the self through the female energies. We express and project through the masculine energy. The patterning for our personality is received through the utilization of father's energy.

The patterns of self expression from father are made possible through the organizing of energy residing in the sub conscious part of the mind that corresponds to the solar plexus chakra.

Beneath the ribs and at the top of the solar plexus, resides the lower causal body. This is where psychic abilities, perception, and the higher emotional qualities of consideration for someone outside of yourself reside.

As the heart chakra above this area begins to open, your thinking changes. You begin to think of yourself as more than a human being. You begin to understand that you are a part of the whole of humanity. That they are your family. You begin to understand that you are in relationship with all human beings, and that you owe. It is time to become aware of what is going on for the life existing here, and to make a contribution towards bettering it. To Master a higher form of Spirituality becomes a driving desire.
You become aware that your life and the way you live it has an influence on all others. Things have to change and become more meaningful.

It is during this time of that we are driven to go out on quest. Life is too mundane. Connection to a higher form of spirituality begins. We have to find our own holiness and relate that to God, and in the doing, find a way to resolve the Nature of God. This journey is fraught with loneliness, because there are not many people doing it. The heart has to learn about this. It can take lifetimes. And so, we begin to seek others on the same lonely path that climbs towards a mountaintop.

Connection to a higher form of spirituality involves changing the energies of the higher mind and the lower soul body. When the heart chakra is activated, energy begins to flow between the solar plexus and the heart chakra. The lower causal body area in between them activates, and picks up the energy of the mind, while the area just above the heart chakra picks up the lower soul energies. A new stage of development has begun. This is a slow process that takes many, many lifetimes.

The throat chakra gradually becomes stimulated by these developing energies, and it begins to open, making way for the higher and lower Nature to blend.

Someday, when the throat chakra is completely open, the person will know that they are entirely responsible for creating their own destiny. They will know that they are not a victim of circumstances. They will begin to take charge of who they are while still contributing to the heart of humanity in some way. This is the path of the Devotee, whose task it is to transmute lower desires into higher desires.

At this point, the feeling nature of the emotions and the feeling nature of the soul become stimulated, and begin to work together.
The energy for this process is given through the naval, spleen, and throat chakras.

As the heart and throat chakra energies unite, the third eye, the chakra located in the center of the forehead, begins to open as this kind of consciousness begins to streams through the systems. A vortexing of energy takes place between the higher mind, the lower mind, and it is at this point that the mind of the soul body begins to change the conscious thinking process of the person's personality. Which is under the influence of your father's sub conscious programming of you.

The work on the reprogramming of the sub conscious mind begins in order to achieve this. The sub conscious mind has to be changed, so that the heart, throat, and third eye chakras can work together in harmony. As the subconscious programming changes, it allows for the heart, throat, and third eye chakras to work together to develop stronger and stronger energy patterns between them.

When the vortex of energies going between the three of them are strong enough, the energy arcs down and picks up the solar plexus energy and blends them all. The new energies begin to go into the liver and spleen energy meridians, and a gradual purification of the liver and spleen takes place over a long, long period of time as the Masculine Nature of your life expands and changes.

When the solar plexus energy is picked up, we begin to understand our ORGANIC relationship with God. With that understanding in tow, we begin to work with the removal of not only the energy blocks in the sub conscious, we begin to remove them from our unconscious as well.

Removing blocks from the unconscious requires strong, active soul expansion. The soul is the part of us that understands expanded time frames past religious points of view on the subject. The soul is the oldest part of the self that has access to our unconscious. As these blocks are removed, the energy is freed to flow down into the spleen and naval chakra so that it can begin to transmute our regeneration and reproduction system from a sexual system to a Spiritual system.

When the brow chakra is open enough, the person's reproductive and regeneration systems change to accommodate the faster, purer energies. The person has evolved to the point that they only desire spiritual energies to run through those systems. One might say only the higher energies of what humans perceive as sexual energy.

Oneness with the Divine Self is experienced.

The gradual acceptance of knowing they can stay in, and have peace about their desire to stay in the new spiritual energies, releases the energy, and it spins up into the crown chakra, and at the same time, down into the root chakra, activating the person's psychic circuits, and creating a halo around their crown chakra, their head, reminiscent of the Buddha's topknot and the Christ's halo, once the chakras have completed their alignment with one another. These results take many lifetimes. And that evolvement and involution is what we are working to achieve on planet Earth.

The internal God now knows that they have to deal with accepting that they cannot use their Will in any way to interfere with or to violate another being.

The external God, in rapport with the internal God, has to come to accept that it will have to deal with the pure, new energies on a regular, permanent basis from then on, and accept the physical limitations that might bring. It takes many lifetimes to accomplish all this, to get to this place, because so much purifying of the self has to be done throughout all the parts of us.

At all times our planet is receiving energies that encourage our evolution and involution, the great spiral of life, mirrored by the genetic coding within us in each cell of our being. The different waves of energy that we receive from the Cosmos encourage the opening of certain chakras at differing amounts of time in order to maintain balance so that we do not implode or explode.

The opened crown chakra is composed of the opened psychic circuits that directly connect to the spinning Cosmic chakras around the crown chakra.

So, now we have come full circle in the process. We came from the Cosmos, and we will return to it each life time, carrying the essence of who we are into new places of discovery. For energy never dies, it just changes its form time after time.

Etheric Web Healing Ritual

Take a spiritual stance of some kind. If you can't do it physically, imagine yourself doing it. You can get someone to take a stance for you, too. But remember, the more you can do yourself, the more powerful the healing. Some things can't be healed by just imagining. Some need witnesses and mirroring.

Imagine you are diving deep down into the Earth. Go down until you are diving through earthy red clay. As you dive, feel the Earth stripping the negative away from you. Then, turn and fly back up to the Earth's surface and stand on the surface of it. Spread your arms out in thanksgiving for the cleanliness you now have. Your feet are like roots in the Earth, and you and the Earth are both glad. (Now you are in alignment with each other) This won't last long.

Look down in front of you. You have brought back a container of beautiful, dark red Earth mud with you. Close your eyes and go to your etheric web and find any rents and tears. Surprise! You took the mud with you. Begin using the luscious, easily molded mud to repair any rents or tears. Very soon, this window of opportunity will close. It only lasts about three minutes. (The word luscious was used on purpose, as it is a word indicating a lovely fat content- this mud has the healing energies provided by the Earth's oils.)

You may not be finished, so you will have to come back another time and work on the rest of it. Wait at least three days before you try this ritual again, for the Earth Elements do not get in alignment with you at your beck and call.

What you can do it to make a habit of checking your etheric web for any problems and getting familiar with where they are located, so that when the elements (Cosmic and Earth) allow you to work there, you won't have to spend time locating the areas to be healed. You can go right to them and set to work. Always thank the Earth and Cosmic forces when you end the ritual. And state, "Let this healing be done in the highest good of all."

A Meditation Technique for Balancing the Colors and Elements.

Take your time doing this meditation.

Imagine yourself standing on the top of a small hill. It is a sunny, warm day and the sky is blue. Down below you is a beautiful tree overlooking a small stream of clear water. On the other side of the stream is a smooth, grassy plain. Walk down to the tree and stand under it. Then step into the stream. Hear the water talking and running over the small, smooth pebbles in the bottom of it. Cross the stream and walk on the silky grass.

See a rainbow off in the distance. The rainbow comes closer and closer. It is touching the ground. Walk into the rainbow. It is like walking into a cloud. Walk through the colors, red, orange, yellow, green, blue, indigo, and violet. Then step out the other side.

See yourself shaking off the excess colors you don't need, like a dog shakes off water after it has been in a stream. Look around at the mountains and trees off in the distance. See the flowers growing all around you.

The rainbow has gone. Turn and walk back leisurely through the grass and across the stream. Stand by the tree for a moment and thank it. Walk back up the small hill you were standing on when you started. Look around the valley below. See all of its beauty. Notice how good you feel. Release any excess energies. Give thanks. Go your way in peace.

The atoms and molecules in our bodies are traceable to the stars across the universe that have lived out their lives manufacturing their Elements and from which new generations start to form.

Putting yourself out to understand this makes dying much easier. The ultimate separation is overseen by the higher masculine nature. It takes the higher masculine nature to do this process.

It is faster moving and contains the concepts that reside within the spheres that reside past the speed of light.

When we abide by the laws of space and time, and its different realities, on Earth we go through two Initiations, one coming onto the planet, one leaving the planet. We dress in our physical body and we undress and leave it behind for the earth to claim again. We move on.

The Colors and Elements, all energies, vibrate differently in the dark than in the light. Sending someone Light is not the same thing as sending them Love. Light comes through the mental body and is attached to few elemental leanings. Love comes from the heart chakra, and contains both Light and Dark. It is sent along through the developed character energies of the person emitting the energies. That's the purpose of learning about different kinds of love energies.

On a personality level, too much Light-electric - too much father- too much motion in all its forms. ADD in children, nervous, can't sit still, constant talking, too positive, can't accept reality.

Too much magnetism – Dark – magnetism – mother - doesn't want to move or make any motion, depression, catatonia, speechless, sad, weepy, negative, accepts too much reality.

Learn to pay attention to the physical manifestations of these energies expressing throughout any energy system and it becomes possible to easily and quickly correct many energy overbalances.

Earth Chakras

The Earth is round and it Spins. Because of this, and other reasons, when Light hits the Earth, the Earth has different ratios of color and elemental energies that stay constant in the different places on it. The equator has a very different light spectrum than the North Pole. Some places have more of the light spectrum, others have less.

The people living in those two very different places would utilize the colors and elemental energies very differently. So we have whole cultures of human beings experiencing and expressing Life in very different ways from each other.

The Earth has many chakras. Where we live on Earth can slow down or advance our particular evolution. Souls come in to live in a certain place and environment to advance or slow down their evolvement.
Each culture has different levels of evolvement developing around each of Earth's chakras. Earth chakras carry energies that affect people negatively or positively. You may want to stay there, or move to another area.

If someone leaves and you wonder where they are, you might send them our cosmic address.

¬ Earth
  ] Solar System
  ] Milky Way Galaxy-we lie 30,000 light years away from its center-our neighbor is Andromeda, the great spiral, And Andromeda is the galaxy next door. It and Earth and a smattering of smaller galaxies make up the "Local Group"
  ] The Local Group consists of the Virgo Super Cluster.
  ] We are one of many thousands of galaxies that make up the Virgo Supercluster which forms a tiny portion of the hundreds of millions of galaxies in our Universe.

The Seven Rays

My great grandfather was a
satisfied man
Contented in every way
Such was the course of his
everyday life
'til he heard of the seven rays

Every modern man, in the back of
his mind
Has a problem to face
He wants security for the home in
his head
All he needs is the seven rays

And when you think about
tomorrow
What goes through your mind?
Now don't nobody get uptight
Do you think that that we can put
up
With this ---- one more night

All you need is just six more rays

Take one beam of light
Prism acquire
Break the white light down
Seven rays appear

One, Red, the ruler seeking
freedom

Two, Gold, the father seeking
unity

Three, Orange, the thinker seeking
understanding

Four, Yellow, the poet seeking
harmony

Take the seven rays
Pure as fire
Focus anywhere
White light will appear

Five, Green, the scientist seeking
truth

Six, blue, the disciple seeking
goodness

Seven, indigo, the artist seeking
beauty

This may sound like a bunch of
trumped up words
But we keep no secrets today
The only hope for you is in your
brothers, my friend
All you need is just six more rays

Songwriters: John Siegler and Todd
Rundgren
The Seven Ray Lyrics Copyright
Warner/Chapell Music. Inc.